*The Wolfboy
of Rego Park*

Jeffrey Wengrofsky

Copyright © 2023 Jeffrey Wengrofsky

Published Exclusively and Globally by Far West Press

All rights reserved. No part of this book may be reproduced in any form or by any electronic or mechanical means, including information storage and retrieval systems, without written permission from the publisher or author, except in the case of a reviewer, who may quote brief passages in a review. Scanning, uploading, and electronic distribution of this book or the facilitation of such without the permission of the publisher is prohibited. Your support of the author's rights is appreciated.

This is a work of fiction. All names, characters, businesses, places, events, and incidents are either the products of the author's imagination or used in a fictitious manner. Any resemblance to actual persons, living or dead, or actual events is purely coincidental.

www.farwestpress.com

First Edition

ISBN 979-8-9858067-8-6

Printed in the United States of America

Table of Contents

Preface........Why I am Burying Myself in this Book
Chapter 1......................The Wolfboy of Rego Park
Chapter 2....................Three Vampirous Vignettes
Chapter 3....................Escaping the Eighth Grade*
Chapter 4......................The Beat Down at CBGB*
Chapter 5..........................A problem with nudity.
Chapter 6....................You'll Always Be an Asshole
Chapter 7................................Who Wants Some?
Chapter 8..........................I was a Teenage Marxist
 (or The Importance of Following Baseball)
Chapter 9............................Requiem for a Tenor
Chapter 10..........Take the Last Train to Auschwitz:
 The Trouble with Trains

Why I am Burying Myself in this Book

The late Lionel Ziprin, Z'L—mystic, (Beat) poet, neighbor, teacher, and friend—once wrote a one-thousand-page poem, arguably the longest of the species, and shipped it off to President Eisenhower along with a note instructing him to tranche it out to soldiers fighting communism in Korea for protection. (Aside from its metaphysical properties, a poem that long might stop a bullet.) In a return letter, Ike sloughed it off, politely reminding Lionel of the Establishment Clause. Following Lionel, I hope that this cache of folly will provide welcome distraction and companionship, if not protection, along your sometimes worrisome, nettlesome, irksome, and/or somewhat hazardous sojourns among the phantasms of "space-time." (It's always better to be fore-armed than under-armed, my dear friends.)

Freud wrote somewhere—maybe everywhere—something like trying to know what is real is the hardest thing we can do. Thanks to Willie Crane, Leslie Hodgkins, Simcha Gottlieb, Eugene Robinson, Kailas Elmer, Ethan Minsker, and Faigie Turner for encouraging this delusion. All blame, however, is mine alone.

Two chapters appeared previously in different form: "The Beat Down at CBGB" was published by *Trebuchet* and "Escaping the Eighth Grade" was published by *Psycho Moto Zine* and *Ozy*.

This book is dedicated to my mother, Malka Cohen Wengrofsky (1942-2004), OBM, wherever she may be.

The Wolfboy of Rego Park

Distantly utopian in concept and gargantuan in scale, modernist residential developments featuring identical buildings, stacks of apartments, common seating areas, and modest grassy patches have provided a none too exotic backdrop to most of my oil-soaked existence.

At the time, dad worked full-time for the U.S. Post Office and at a paint store on weekends, mom tended to my little brother, and I was tasked with walking to kindergarten in a building not more than a hundred feet from the one that we lived in. The spring sun shone warm and generous, and the air was fresh with the scent of the earth reawakening. Little yellow bees flitted about the heads of dandelions and danced among the crabgrasses.

As I approached school, I heard my classmates in the schoolyard, presumably playing, as usual. When I came closer, however, I saw that they were, in fact, screaming in terror, taken hostage by an enormous dog, perhaps a German shepherd, holding fierce ground between the kids and the safety of the classrooms.

Drawing up from behind, I barked at the dog. After a moment, it stopped barking and turned to me, twisting its head and pulling back into a deep growl. I turned and took off running. It chased me down in no time, sinking its fangs through my thin spring coat and deeply into my arm. I fell to the sidewalk. Savage jaws snapped above my face. Then, the dog turned and galloped out of view, vanishing as suddenly as it had appeared.

"Are you OK?" A teacher picked me up, adding: "It's a good thing that I came when I did."

My teacher stepped out from behind her and was

having none of it: "To set the record straight, I was the one who scared the dog off."

"No, you weren't. It left when it saw me shake my pocketbook."

"That's not true. The dog left when I yelled at it." My teacher inspected my arm, which leaked red through the ripped coat sleeve, and pulled my coat off.

"*They always* run when they see my pocketbook," said the other teacher, quietly and firmly.

"No...they...don't..." snapped my teacher, whisking me into her classroom.

Later that night, mom came into the room I shared with my brother and softly woke me up. She checked my bandage and took me by the hand. A police officer sat at the kitchen table. He asked me what the dog looked like. I told him. He spoke with heavy blocks of wood that spilled onto the floor: "rabies," which are like bugs, "a boy in Rego Park," dogs, and "like a wolf." Mom turned to me: we were going to see a doctor. Then the officer asked if I'd ever been in a police car. I didn't say anything. He said he would take me and my dad to look for the dog in a few days. Dad whispered saccharinely: "We're going to take a ride in a *real* police car." Pointing toward the ceiling and rotating a finger, he softly imitated a siren.

Mom tucked me back into bed, kissed my forehead, and wished me "sweet dreams." I tried stitching it all together: the boy, the dog, Rego Park, and the rabies bugs. Then I saw him—The Wolfboy—on all fours, his head ripping into a garbage bag behind a restaurant. I tried to tell him that I understood him, that he didn't have to be alone anymore, but he stared back through the big, blank, black eyes of an angry insect, like a wasp. Rising awkwardly to his hind limbs, revealing filthy belly and hairy limbs, he staggered toward me more horrible than expected. I turned to run, like I ran that morning, but I could only move in slow motion. The Wolfboy ran beside me, snapping jagged teeth, then ripped flesh from my arm, which blazed in a fountain of blood.

I woke up in bed. Opening my eyes, I was relieved to be back home. I'd been laying on my bad arm, which felt prickly. Mom gently nudged: "It's time to get up." My kid brother was already in the kitchen, eating Farina and grape jelly with a big, silly grin. And a blob of purple jelly gliding down his chin.

As mom poured hot water into my bowl, she told me that I was going to the doctor instead of going to school. Brother would come along as well, of course, because he was too small to be home alone.

***

Shining a small flashlight in my eyes, the doctor reassured, "It's a good thing that you came down when you did." Then he turned to mom in a heavy way, which made his words fall down. Removing my bandages and examining my arm, he resumed, absent-mindedly, "Good...yes... everything is going to be... alright." My arm looked back at me from a pair of scabby holes. The doctor cleaned the holes, which stung a bit, and re-bandaged the arm. Then he turned his back and opened a cupboard. My brother was fidgeting around in the corner. I flipped him a funny face, which made him giggle.

Taking my hand, mom told me to look at her and to be completely still: "After the doctor, we're going to the toy store. Think about what you want." As I thought about it, I could feel a sharp pain in my stomach. "Hold him still," repeated the doctor. Mom held me tight: "Look at me. Look at mommy and tell me what you want." The pain in my belly was back. "Almost done. Be a nice boy and hold still just a little longer." Closing my eyes, I saw the doctor, my mom, my brother, and me, holding still. In twenty-one intervals over the next several months, the doctor stuck an enormous needle into my stomach, and I would try to keep from moving. Sometimes I'd get a Matchbox or a Hot Wheels car afterward.

***

That night, I sank deeply into bed wondering whether it was already too late for me. I felt the bugs running around my arm under the skin and I felt them fighting against the doctor's poison. There was a civil war in my arm, and I was the battlefield. If the medicine was too strong, wouldn't it kill me too? And what would happen if it wasn't strong enough and the bugs won? Would I turn on my family? I saw my brother fast asleep, drooling into his pillow. Was he safe with me around? There was a terrible itch in my throat, and I couldn't make a sound. Mouth full of hair, I coughed dryly. Could not breathe. Reaching deep into the back of my mouth, I pulled out a long, hairy strand. My arm was thick with fur. I wanted to rip it off and throw it out the window.

When I woke up in the morning, my arm was still bandaged and sore. As I brushed my teeth, I fearfully stared at myself in the bathroom mirror, studying my eyes. Running my fingers across my scalp, I surveyed my head for bulbous antennae. Finally, I felt around for bugs under my bandages and down my arm.

The other kids ran away when I entered the schoolyard that morning. A girl told me that her mother said that I shouldn't be in school: "Why don't you just play with the other dogs?" I tried to tell her what the doctor said, but she didn't care: "Did you hear about that other boy?" Everyone knew about the Wolfboy and soon everyone would know about me! She barked and her friends joined in, barking and imitating dogs. My arm throbbed, as if the bugs were activated. Why were bugs in the dog that bit me? Were wolfbugs in my head? I listened for inner voices, but the only dog sounds I heard that day came from the other kids.

**

A few days later, dad and I got in the back of a police cruiser to look for the dog. I was surprised by how many stray dogs we saw. They were everywhere, especially under the highway. Could I only see them now because I was becoming one of them? I tried to meet their eyes, but they were disinterested, and none of them were the dog that bit me. I ran my tongue over my teeth to check if any were long or sharp.

That night, I found myself back in the backseat of the police car, without the police and without my dad. The car steered itself, slowly and confidently. Enormous trees stretched upwards from the middle of streets, their stalks reaching through the clouds, with leaves so lavish and full as to obscure the sun. Wolves with swollen black wasp eyes and antennae as broad as moose antlers roamed in thick packs. Some dogs sprouted wings and hovered awkwardly in mid-air, their tails wagging happily. Dogfaces stared out of apartment windows. Some smoked cigars. One had its hair in curlers. Of course, I knew where I was. "This…" I self-narrated, "This…must be Rego Park."

Three Vampirous Vignettes

Vignette One: Are There Any Vampires in the House?

After decades of coating the ships of the Brooklyn Navy Yard with lead-infused paint, grandpa came down with cancer. We—mom, dad, brother, and I—visited him at a large, public hospital in south Brooklyn, witnessing, in increments, his slow, yet certain, slide into the grave.

It was at the end of one of these visits, so late at night that the whole world was dim even with the lights on, as if a gauze had been placed over reality to help it fall asleep. Official visiting hours had drawn to a close and we took the elevator to the lobby, which was crowded, so crowded in fact, that we could not have politely made our exit if we wanted to. Instead of leaving the lobby, hospital visitors stood around, as if under a collective hypnosis. Ensnared in the foot traffic, we became curious as to its cause.

Being that I was young, I was way too short to see much at first, except the tall backs and long wool coats of adults. I noticed that the lobby had a polished tile floor, and then became somehow aware of a high ceiling with a mezzanine, an oblong information desk, and, in the center of it all, a large glass enclosure—like a fish tank—with three teenagers inside sitting cross-legged. A doctor entered the tank and spoke briefly with the teens, who, spurning his medical advice, began chanting in a language I could not understand. The crowd parted, providing the doctor a lane to walk over to the information desk.

The hospital intercom explained that the teens, keen on dying, chanted to increase the flow of their blood, which spurted from them as they rhythmically intoned, sloppily gurgling onto the floor of the glass enclosure, where it collected, coagulating. The voice continued, shifting from cold diagnosis to troubled plea: "Are there any vampires in the hospital? All vampires, please report to the lobby. We have another set of suicides." The teens, it was understood, were members of a suicide cult, then the latest fad among trendy youth. And although vampires were not to be trusted, they had a right to make a living, so to speak, and the spoilage of good blood was considered wasteful, as we are always in times of scarcity.

Lobby lights were turned off to allow the vampires to proceed without interference. The room was now filled by a darkness doubly dimmed by the absence of artificial light and the still-dimming ultra-late-night hour. Chanting grew louder, then sharply plaintive, as if the teens were crying their blood out.

A woman's scream, a dagger, pierced the air, and was soon followed by a strained whimper. Then another and another, until a whirlwind of wails filled the pitch and palpable darkness. Excited by the supply of fresh blood and emboldened by the dark, the vampires were loose in the crowd and more numerous than the hospital expected. I would come to later understand this as a "feeding frenzy." I withdrew from the situation by closing my eyes.

***

This was the first of many vampire-centered nightmares that spooked me solid from age seven to twelve. Usually, they centered around the fire escape beside the window next to my bed. Vampires—male and female—would drift up from the street or from a nearby rooftop to land on the fire escape before seeking entry through my window. Sometimes the sound of them tapping would wake me up. Opening my eyes just slightly, I would see them pressing their faces against the glass.

From grandma's third-story window, as we were

often there, I often saw ghouls perched atop the verdigris-stained spires of St. Mary's Church—spires that stabbed the night sky like fangs—or gathered on its deep rooftop, grazing sloppily on organ meat while murmuring eerily, like at a conference for well-attired vultures of the night. A few would float above the church, suspended silently in the still, late-night air, occasionally resting on streetlamps. Staring into their undulating black mass, all crushed velvet and cashmere, pale eyes would eventually drift back to meet mine. Better not to look and to not be seen. Once, at a family function, I recall having had the misfortune of walking in on one that had wandered into my grandma's bedroom. As surprised as I was by it, the vampire spun, nervously, with eyes hypnotic and overpowering. I froze and lost consciousness.

Vignette Two: Hell in the Hallway

A family is home in their apartment at night. Their heavy steel front door is all that protects them from known and unknown horrors.

An unholy presence/at the door/KNOCK/silence/an unholy presence/death hunting for life/dank coffin/**POUNDING**/an unholy presence/steel groans/hinges buckle.

Silence.

The will of the stronger/top lock/opens/lower lock/opens/death/door opens slowly/**screaming**/ bloody death/pale eyes know your name/fangs of a snake/hiss/louder than sound/death/ **SCREAMING**/ burning eyes/death/screaming/your death/red/bloodlust: **THE VAMPIRE**.

Screaming.

My parents had no idea what had turned their son into shrieking violet. I could neither see nor hear them. I was not among them. After a bit, they saw that I was transfixed on the TV, which showed a preview of a vampire movie from waking life, with subway stations, hallways, florescent stairwells, elevators, and apartment doors.

They turned it off. Caught between realities, inconsolably stalled between floors, I slept with my folks that night, much to their chagrin.

Vignette Three: With Swollen Limbs and a Heavy Heart

More than just seeing medical gear while on trips to see grandpa, I also saw a good bit of it at my friend Tracey's apartment in the building next to mine. Tracey Earl was 50% black, 50% Jewish, and 100% hemophiliac. Half of the time, he'd run around with the rest of us kids, playing stickball, tag, football, basketball ("Earl the Pearl"), and kick-the-can on the parking lots and grassy bits between our buildings. The other half of the time, he was in bed recuperating from the dings and pings of play with limbs bulbously swollen from internal bleeding and platelets oozing into his arm. Instead of going out, we'd dialog on primary sources from the standard repertoire (*Captain America, The Fantastic Four, Black Panther, Power Man & Iron Fist,* and *The Hulk*) and classic television (*The Lone Ranger* and *Batman*), stage battles with green plastic army men, and enact smash up derbies with vehicles we built from Lego.

We also made up our own superheroes. Tracey's hero was "Super Furry." He looked like a little tangled tuft of hair with big feet. And his superpower came from a sound he made that could levitate him, repel an opponent, or shatter glass. My superhero was called "Neptunite." He could fly, but he flew low to the ground and regrettably slowly, because he was super heavy. You see, Neptunite was made from a dense substance at the solid-as-fuck core of Neptune, the blue gas giant. His main superpower was that this density made him unbreakable, so he could be dropped down on super villains, to their vast detriment.

When we'd get into it, Tracey would mimic the sound of Super Furry, and, invariably, his downstairs neighbors would bang up to his floor. Spurred on and in mindful enjoyment of the behavioral latitude his disability provided, Tracey would answer with the Super Furry sound and jump on his bed as if levitating. Sometimes I dropped on super villains, to their vast detriment. We could be such brats.

Once, when Tracey came over to my family's apartment for lunch, he, my little brother, and I, played a game in which we opened our mouths to gross each other out while trying to crack each other up. My brother laughed so hard that he tipped over backward, and his butt went through the rattan backing of his chair. With the sorry realization that we'd really damaged the kitchen set, we sheepishly ended the game and nervously awaited parental judgement.

***

I asked Tracey if playing with the kids outside was worth the pain and trouble of recovery. After all, as you can see, we had a lot of fun inside, and other kids were often problematic. His mom came quietly into the room. After a beat, Tracey emphatically declared that he was a normal kid and had absolutely no intention of hanging up his sneakers. I asked if he needed or wanted my blood.

His mom laughed, "No, that's not how it works," and offered us cookies.

"But where did the blood come from?"

His mom answered, "Some people give away their blood."

"Is it painful?"

"Not at all," his mom laughed, assuredly, telling me that she'd done it many times.

"Why would someone give their blood to someone they didn't know?"

Tracey's mom also had an answer for this one: "Because a good person cares about other people, even people they don't know."

Tracey drew my attention to a portrait of his father hanging on their living room wall, pointing out that wherever he went in the room, his father's eyes followed, watching over him like a guardian angel. It certainly seemed that way to me, although it also seemed like his father's eyes watched me as well, which Tracey quickly dismissed. After all, I never met his father; he had died before I even met Tracey.

When his mom left the room, I briefed Tracey on matters too serious and grave for a mom to handle: the vampire dreams and that movie. The bending door and yielding locks were particularly concerning to Tracey. After all, he and his mom kept blood in the house. If the vampires got wind of the cache of blood, and Tracey was attacked, he'd never stop bleeding. We did the only thing two adolescent kids could do: we laid a trap for the vampires, with help from Super Furry and Neptunite, of course.

***

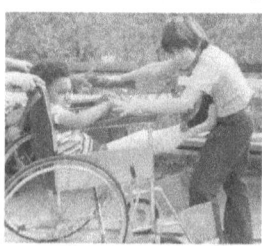 

Training for the Battle Royale.

Weeks later, waking to pee. Returned to bed. Crickets called to one other from under my pillow, scratching out million-year-old melodies. A siren answered, distantly.

Rising/resounding through canyons of brick and glass/the sound of Super Furry/explosions/screaming/terror/**my room in red light**/a wall of red windows across the street/**the high sign**.

It was go-time. I opened my bedroom window slowly to not rouse my brother, stepping out onto the fire escape in my pajamas and a t-shirt. Cool iron rails, slightly wet, creaked just slightly beneath bare feet. Drawing in the humid summer air, I scanned the night, watching for Neptunite to fall from the sky, and steeled myself for battle.

***

Tracey Earl died a few years later from complications related to HIV.

Escaping the Eighth Grade

Eighth grade was the worst: my other grandfather died, I was publicly mocked by the first girl I ever asked out, home life was sketchy, my habit of talking to myself grew into a chorus, and school nearly turned deadly. Along the way, I had a bar mitzvah. Adulthood was off to a shaky start.

School days began with dodging an assortment of jokers trying to spill out the contents of my loose-leaf notebook and more. First up was Bobby Graves, a chubby, pale Irish kid who resembled a little white bear. Bobby would hide behind parked cars holding a piece of dogshit, which he'd try to put in my face. It wasn't personal, but it definitely made him laugh, which winded him and made it easier to run away. To be sure, Bobby received his share of daily grief, and the bad energy flows down the social hierarchy, sometimes manifesting as a piece of crap in someone's face. Bobby also liked to spit in his hand and fling it at people, and soon, everyone was doing it to everyone. There was a lot of spit in the air that year.

First period was called "homeroom" because, I would later note, following Morrissey, that "barbarism begins at home." After attendance was called, George Della-Calce, a spit-balling Italian-American kid with more than his share of the Vinnie Barbarino gene, would try to drag me into a storage room at the far end of the classroom. If he succeeded, he'd punch me in the face until I cried. Eventually, I learned to cry when he got me back there before he started punching. This would frustrate George because, I suppose, he enjoyed the physicality of bullying but lacked the heart for serious sadism.

George was one of several in my class who'd been left back a year or more owing to having committed undisclosed sins upon their previous classmates. If my school was like a prison, these kids were like "lifers"—big and bad to the bone. They'd been through all the system could do to them and were defiantly serving time until, at sixteen, they could legally dropout. The school had pronounced the execution of a year of their lives, and they spat back—sometimes literally. It's hard to say why people do what they do; how much of it is cultural, psychological, biological, or the malign handiwork of a demon wandering among humanity since the age of Cain.

Mixing the kids together was official pedagogy, a way of bringing up the lifers, but what happened is that they brought everyone down to their level. Sharks chewed chunks from schools of minnows. Kids were intimidated in class and beaten in the corridors. The meekest, like "Richie" West, were destroyed. He'd wretch back and forth in his chair, mumbling and fussing with his hands even when no one was near him.

About halfway through the spring term, we were asked to write short stories. A small, nervous kid who talked to himself, I had a lively if not wholly original, imagination. Although I didn't always do my homework, it was fun to jot down a few fantasies concerning a character called "James Bomb." Unlike his suave namesake, *Meester Bomb*—as he was referred to by chattering nemeses—had no sex life and never survived an adventure fully intact. Actually, one of his signatures, which had made him an effective agent, was a complete disregard for his own safety. To wit, his face was once peeled off by ghoulish captors, who tossed it out a window. To their astonishment, Bomb simply jumped out of the window, caught his face like a frisbee, shattered a few limbs on impact, limped away, and painfully re-stitched it himself when he got home. In my mind, a real spy was covered in scars and scabs, lacked a good bit of hair, suffered from terrible nightmares, and had the decrepit grin of a hockey player. Bomb walked jagged and winced often from his accumulating injuries. A chart of his jerry-rigged anatomy would've captivated Rube Goldberg. His foes would often remind Bomb that he was the ugliest spy of all time—a distinction he embraced. Each morning, he greeted his face with laughter at once scornful and triumphant. Bomb's other key strength was his uncanny ability to calculate weak spots in glass windows and ricochet trajectories for bullets. His only companion was a Beretta he'd painstakingly recalibrated for phenomenal accuracy.

As one of just a handful of students to actually complete assignments, I was asked to read my stories to the class. George actually liked James Bomb, never understanding that he was the inspiration for at least one of the humanoid monsters that Bomb shot repeatedly in the face. From that time on, George faded out as a tormentor, though my designation as a potential victim lingered on.

Although at that point I hadn't read more than fifty pages of any book, I liked them. When school offered students a selection of cheap pulp paperbacks at a group discount, I was able to get my folks to fork over the cash—maybe two or three bucks for two or three books. As it turned out, I was the only student in the class to order books, so my teacher returned the money to me. Unfortunately, she did it in front of everyone. Ernie Jones and Angel Dupree, Bronx "lifers" whose violent behavior had already led to their being left back at least once, took note. Neither paid any attention in class and both frequently interrupted the teacher. They sat in the back menacingly, but hadn't sought me out before. By my reckoning, each was about six feet tall, which was about a foot taller than I was then.

When our English teacher walked into the hall to chat with a colleague in the hallway, Ernie and Angel hauled me to the back of the classroom and wrestled away the money. Dissatisfied with such easy bounty, they picked me up and pushed me completely outside the window, three stories above the street, holding me by my wrists.

> Our hero, pushed to the brink of annihilation, dangled miles above the teeming metropolis. Bomb could feel a strong pulse in his feet and sensed cold emptiness below. He looked up to see his foes, their faces grotesquely distorted in laughter; monsters engorged with malicious delight. Below, cars were like little toys and people looked like ants, unaware of the drama unfurling above them. The city churned. Bomb strained in the hands of the monsters, yet beneath him yawned the hungry abyss. He wanted to get away from his captors, yet their grip was all that kept him from being smashed by the planet. And his trusty gun—his only true friend—was nowhere to be found. The street undulated like the face of a lake ready to swallow him. The sky was blue, and the yellow sun shone on, distantly watching the scene unfold.

My teacher returned. Ernie and Angel pulled me back up into the room in full view. The three of us were brought to the principal's office. Ernie and Angel were suspended for a week. My parents were dissuaded from pursuing further action by a principal concerned about traumatizing Ernie and Angel, who were identified as "at-risk."

When Ernie and Angel returned from their week of suspension, they were real mad—especially Angel.

He'd wait for me after school and try to grab me. I recall him coming up from behind and, pressing a knife into my face, whispering, "Don't make me cut you." I could feel the blade make a dimple in my cheek. From then on, he'd occasionally make a throat-cutting gesture if I accidentally looked his way in class. An angel of the unholy sort; fire and bullets and even the loss of a year of his life could not faze him.

After a time, it occurred to me that, rather than face Angel, I could escape by cutting the last period or two of school, so I often did. Compared with the cunning and astounding aim of James Bomb, this was, of course, a pedestrian solution, but it got me out of the eighth grade.

The Beat Down at CBGB

"Do you have a history of epilepsy?"

She held a bottle of smelling salts under my nose. I took another whiff. Whoa. My vision populated with blue and red and purple blotches.

She repeated herself, "Do you have a history of epilepsy?"

"No." The world slowly drew into focus.

"You had a seizure."

My head hurt. I was seated on a little chair at the front of CBGB, the infamous punk rock club, by the side of the entrance, near the office. I could hear a band playing. For years afterwards I used to joke that "The Outpatients knocked me out," but that's not quite what happened.

She came back. "We need to call your parents so they can get you."

"No....I'm fine." I started to stand up.

"What's your number? You passed out and now we can't let you go. Your parents have to pick you up."

She left.

The door guy came over and said, "You're not leaving. Give her your number."

What was I going to do?

There would be hell to pay. Worse than whatever had happened, I'd have to answer for it and make it somehow alright. My dad hated everything about hardcore—and I mean every single thing: the music, the style, its subcultural character and radical refusal of social norms, and that it was mine. One of the things he hated most was that it was based out of CBGB on the Bowery, New York City's skid row of flop houses—a derelict zone of forgotten dreams and defeated souls set amid broken sidewalks decorated with shattered glass bottles of Thunderbird and Colt

45.

At the time, I was living with my grandma, and there was NO WAY that I could let them call her. Grandma was a worry-wart, and the idea that her grandson was damaged while out in the "forbidden zone" of the East Village would have realized her worst fears. I'd never hear the end of it. Besides, the very idea of her coming into CBGB—which she mockingly referred to as "*Heebie Jeebie*"—was simply outside the realm of concrete possibility. Grandma and CBs didn't really exist on the same plane of existence and bringing them together (though she only lived a few blocks away) would have been a water and oil mix of impossibility that would have collapsed reality as we know it.

So, they called my dad and he came into the club. Our eyes met. I rose silently, and followed him out onto the Bowery. There was a cold reckoning: "Your mother and I work hard so that you and your brother don't have to be in places like this, yet here you are." The verdict, having been given, the inquest began:

"Do you mind telling me what happened?"

"I passed out."

I could sense both of his eyebrows going up, "Are you high?"

"No." It was the truth. I was stone cold sober. Seriously, I was. "Do I have a history of epilepsy? I had a seizure."

Dad had been around the block, and he was not buying it: "Gimme a break. These people suck." He never did mince words. What could I say? How did I get into this stupid situation?

What Was Hardcore Punk?

In the early 1980s, if you were listening for a clarion call of rebellion, a semi-autonomous subculture of wild intellectuality, music as emotion, and the realness of a boot in the face, you heard it in Hardcore. As The Ramones had offered a stripped-down version of rock, hardcore did the same for punk, making it even more primal, manic, and brief. And, as my first great musical love was Black Sabbath, the sound of hardcore resonated with me on a molecular level. Moreover, for a kid like me, who never felt comfortable in mainstream society, connecting to a scene that valorized outsider-ness was a hand-in-glove experience. Hardcore made it clear to me that trying to succeed in mainstream society—which, as a college kid, meant moronic drinking and the conformity of the frat house—was unworthy of time and spirit. Hardcore was a "Great Refusal" of money and sex and popularity, a provocation to the outside world and, when we got together, we burned brightly. "Slam dancing," "moshing," and all that, were a form of rough-housing, usually good-natured, that presented opportunities for bad behavior. Hardcore was risky and dangerous, which was part of its rough-hewn appeal.

Hardcore was made for kids like me by kids like me and it showed: shows and records were intentionally cheap, premiums were placed on passion and authenticity over technique, and the issues broached in the music defined my life. It was "underground" in the sense independent of corporations and virtually hidden from the mass media. Information about "the scene" required tapping into an otherwise invisible network of fliers and 'zines, and then attending shows in squats and other decrepit places deep in the city's nether crevices. Even hearing the music meant trekking to record stores on and around St. Marks Place: Venus, Sounds, Freebeing, and The Rat Cage. Or, if at a matinee, you could pick up the latest from Dave Parsons of Rat Cage Records, who'd

The author as a young monster.

scoot over to CBGB on a skateboard in a dress with a crate of records on his shoulder sporting a 5 o'clock shadow from a pronounced Adam's apple.

Contributing to its mystique as hidden knowledge, many early hardcore bands were well-read, which made the listening a challenge that stoked my intellectual curiosity. The net effect of all this is that I followed literary leads from my records into my studies and came to excel at school for the first time in my life. When I wasn't hanging with punk pals, I crammed ideas into my head. A heady teen, notions of anarchy and socialism, then without voice, sparkled with the exoticism and idealistic promise of an alternative universe. *Maximumrocknroll*, the monthly heartbeat of the international punk underground, under the editorship of Tim Yohannon, a member of the Revolutionary Communist Party, encouraged anarchism, with a few exceptions, like Jeff Bale, whom I criticized. Meanwhile, if you squinted, the East Village of Manhattan could be viewed as a laboratory for realizing anarchism. (When New York City Mayor Dinkins closed Tompkins Square Park for two years, he said it was because the neighborhood was "out of control," and, indeed, it was.) Taken altogether, there was an identity in all this that gave me the courage to do outrageous things that are part and parcel of the glorious folly of youth. My overly pedantic sense of the world—all books and no brawl—would, eventually, run smack dab into a rough physical reality.

New York Skinheads

Where there is a ying, there is also a yang. In the hardcore underworld, extreme ideas—left-wing and right-wing—came to exchange sharp elbows. There were no rules and no rulers, so anything went, including bad behavior. Along with anarchistic "peace punks," New York had skinheads, many of whom had worldviews and lifestyles that were our mirror opposite: many chose religion (Hare Krishna) and some were "straight-edge" (abstaining from drugs, alcohol, and sex). Despite some Nazi fetishism, some skins were black and many of them were Latin, and few were actively hateful of Jews, let alone racist. In short, the skins didn't have a coherent ideology; they just rebelled against the punks. Peace punks would simply lose their minds when Agnostic Front's Roger Miret, a Cuban-American, sang in front of an American flag. The common denominator among New York City skins was a penchant for violence. In the early days, Harley Flanagan of the Cro-Mags and his crew cruised the Bowery with eight-balls in stockings to beat bums and homosexuals. They also sometimes mashed scrawny, bookish, radical punks like me.

Entering CBGB or simply passing by on the Bowery, one could sense danger, which made it all important and exciting, like re-living the Weimar Republic in spikes and black leather. As I'd already encountered some rough times, I accepted it as simply part of the equation, but I was streetwise enough to never make eye contact with Harley or Roger or their closely cropped toadies in DMS. More than once I even used "The Power of The Force" to be invisible to skins in my vicinity. Although I didn't share their views, I respected them for being real, and kept my distance.

During shows, I'd stand to the right of the stage, just outside the pit, or to the left of the stage, close-up, by the monitors, where I got a great view of the band and didn't have to deal with the slam dancing. Back then, skins were disinclined to committing open acts, preferring instead to create a pretense. Being in or near the pit invited bad behavior: pile-ons, sucker punches, tripping, and group attacks. Skinheads were an unfortunate part of the scene, a vestige of the "crooked timber of humanity" that kept humans from paradise.

Back to the Scene of the Crime

When we got home, Dad told me that he'd beat me silly and banish me from his home as well as from grandma's sweet little nest if I shaved my head. Mom warned that she could not control him, which was always unsettling to hear. Surely, many of the punk kids I ran with had already gone through that sort of thing and were squatting. Thin, bespectacled, and asthmatic, I was not cut out for life on the street and I knew it. So, I promised to never join the ranks of the baldies, which was something I didn't want to do, anyway.

The following week, I went on over to the CBGB matinee, same as it ever was. During the intermission between bands, I stepped outside. There, Louis Ramos, a little Afro-Rican kid wearing a torn Sex Pistols t-shirt, engaged me on punk rock esoterica. We prattled on for a while, assessing each other's level of cool and understanding of punk, and became fast friends.

A few months later, Louis confided that our meeting was not mere happenstance. He'd sought me out because he saw the whole sordid affair, and he thought I was "hardcore" for coming back and acting as if nothing had happened. In other words, he thought I was crazy and all-the-more fascinating for it. A week earlier, at The Outpatients show at CBGB, Louis saw me with my homemade Misfits t-shirt, caught in a current, pulled into the pit. And he saw me getting "rabbit punched" in the back of the head by some skinhead. I went down immediately and hard. The crowd parted. I laid on the floor, twitching. No one knew what to do. The skin who hit me came forward, muttering "it was an accident" or some such. My body, lifeless as a sack of potatoes, was half-carried and half-dragged to the front of CBGB. And the band played on.

Anarchy is a return to the natural order. Might makes right. If you are a punk in the pit, you might get hit. The zebra has stripes to confuse lions, but the camouflage only works when they run as a pack. The nail that stands up gets the beat down.

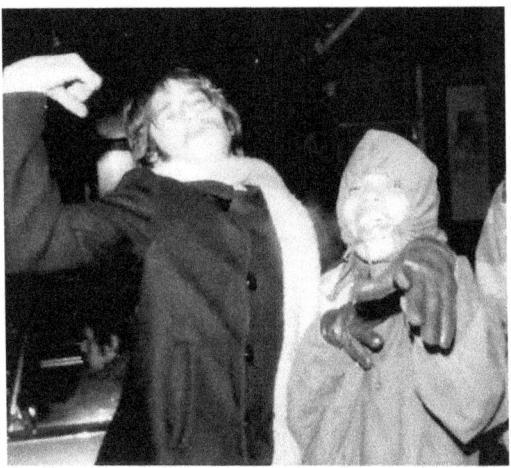

The author and Louis terrorizing the Lower East Side in the way back.

A problem with nudity.

"Does anyone have a problem with nudity?"

A pack of scrawny punks—some near- and one full-on virgin—none of us were prepared for that question. Justina, the only chick in our little crew, herself allegedly deflowered by Johnny Thunders, was the first to think it through: "I'm out. You can go ahead." Entirely put off by the topic, she dismissed the lot of us for even asking. Abraham was quick to join her, and the two left to share that long train trip back to The "boogie down" Bronx. The rest of us—Brett, Louis, Louis's cousin Ray, and me—desperately wanted to do *something*. Besides, the only other suggestion anyone had was wandering around with John Spacely on one of his junkie journeys, which had limited appeal.

It was summertime and St. Marks Place was in its full degenerate glory: punks, drug fiends, radicals, and weirdos set the pace.

Brett and Donny, or, as he preferred to be known, "Donny The Punk," had been pen pals. With friends all over the world, Brett was the most active of us in the international hardcore punk underground. All he could tell us was that Donny was a writer and that he'd done time in prison. Conjoining one of my deepest desires with one of my greatest fears made the invitation worth overlooking plausible issues around "nudity."

We were buzzed in, and the apartment door was ajar when we climbed upstairs. "The door's open. Come in and make yourselves at home. We'll be out in a minute," Donny welcomingly tossed from deep inside the apartment.

A young, tall black skinhead about my age was stomping around in his underwear. With eyes fixed to the floor, he shyly avoided eye contact while scanning the floor for clothing. Without saying a word, he assembled his outfit and bolted out the door.

Donny was next to appear, emerging from a bedroom in the rear, and also in his underwear. A middle-aged white guy of medium height and proportionate weight, his visage was plain in every respect except that he had a mohawk. Pulling up a pair of jeans, he introduced himself: "I'm Donny, although I have also had many other names, among them Robert Martin, R.A. Martin, and Stephen Donaldson." And with that, he launched into a thumbnail version his life story: founding the first LGBTQ+ student club in American history, time in the navy, multiple stints in prison, membership in MENSA, writing a history of homosexuality, and practicing Buddhism.

Donny was the first professional writer I'd ever met, very knowledgeable about the punk scene, and was into Buddhism—a passing interest of mine. I was hooked. He invited us to rummage through a bin of records and put something on. Brett put on Richard Hell and the Voidoids's second record.

An older, saggy Latin woman with the freshness of an ashtray emerged from some dank recess of the back bedroom and whispered in Donny's ear. He whispered back. As he introduced Lisa, a mother of two little kids asleep in a second bedroom, she dropped to her knees in front of him, pulling down the pants he'd just pulled up. By this time, Donny was delving into his idiosyncratic, but intriguing take on Buddhism. As we discussed whether reincarnation matters if the Self is destroyed in the death/rebirthing process, Lisa sucked his cock, not skipping a beat. Albeit I found the emerging scene disquieting, Donny's evident genius kept the conversation rolling. Eventually, as we say, he paused in mid-sentence for a convulsing, eye-rolling, and generally revolting orgasm deep into her throat cavity. Moments later, and restored to his senses, he addressed the group as a gracious host, "Does anyone else want a blowjob?" Fidgeting about, we politely declined, as one might a well-intentioned invitation to share in some well-seasoned shit. Seeing no takers, but convinced of the product, he took a second shot at making the sale: "She's great. I recommend her." With no verbal response, he then resumed discoursing on Buddhism.

Then, leaving Lisa, Louis, Brett, and Ray in conversation, Donny led me on a guided tour of the apartment, beginning with *Urban Combat*, a board game he'd created. Leading me down a hall, he pointed out that the walls were covered with white paper because, as an illegal sublet, he needed to protect them from spontaneous acts of creativity. Drawing me into a bedroom, he beckoned to join him at a window, "My spiritual interests also include 'phallic worship,' which incorporates Hinduism and magic." With that, he showed me a shrine of three plastic dildos on the windowsill: two were small and one was of medium size.

Louis came into the room and gave me a sign that he, Brett, and Ray were going to split, which I took as an opportunity to exchange contact information and say farewell to Donny and Lisa.

Hitting the street, Louis groaned "What do you see in that pervert?"

Imploring open-mindedness, I argued, "That's superficial. He's smart and interesting." I continued, recycling arguments I'd just learned from Donny: "Besides, what's wrong with nudity or sex? They're basic facts of life. Clothes are an illusion."

"He's just a gross, old *maricón*. Think about what he did in front of us." Slowing down to half-speed for emphasis, Louis spelled it out: "He's a grown man twice our age. He should know better. He's a creep."

"What about Lisa?"

"Her kids live with her and that creep, which makes her a double-creep."

I pushed back again: "It doesn't matter what he was doing while he was talking, since it didn't involve us and it was clearly consensual." As I listed some of the cool shit that Donny was into, Louis broke in: "I tell you what – you can hang out with him on your own and, I bet you, he's going to try to fuck you."

***

Over the next couple of months, Donny invited me to see many bands. Louis, Ray, Abraham, and Justina derided every invitation. (Brett lived in Philly.) And yes, Lisa would blow Donny each time I went over there, which was an annoying price for access to an impressive mind.

Flier personal collection of Jeffrey Wengrofsky

Donny was very clear that, no matter how much he liked punk rock, his nickname derived from serving time in prison. As he told me, getting raped in prison is so common, especially for white guys like him—let alone runts like me—that it would happen in any facility I'd be sent to: "It's not the time, it's the company." The key to survival, for him, was keeping his wits. When, during his first prison sentence, it became known that he enjoyed sex with men (he identified as "polymorphously perverse"), it brought on a series of racialized gang rapes. The second time he was imprisoned—this time for threatening to shoot a clinician who told him that he needed to wait a week for herpes treatment—he was, again, faced with gang rape. Having learned, he reached out to a bunch of white former marines, offering to service the lot of them for protection. It worked out well for all and, according to him, polymorphous perversity was a state of mind worth mastering in case dint of raw fate brought me to The Big House. Inmates are divided ethnically, with black, Latin, and white supremacists being the primary affiliations—with no room for Jews—so I'd need to be especially resourceful. "In life," as he put it, with the inflection of a guru, "it is sometimes sapien to be homo." He'd sometimes ask why I thought I liked women when I had no evidence one way or the other: "Being 'straight' seems very confining. It always reminds me of the phrase, 'straight and narrow.'" On release from prison, Donny came to embrace the emerging punk scene, and already had a nickname suitable for many occasions—including advocacy of NAMBLA.

***

Grandma called me into the kitchen. Donny was on the line.

"Hey Jeff. Want to see a show?"

"Sure. Where?"

"In Williamsburg, at The Ship's Mast." Directly across the East River from grandma's place, Williamsburg had hardly begun its long ride into hipsterdom. It was Memorial Day. We—Donny, Lisa, and I—met up at the little bombed-out former trolly house at the base of the Williamsburg Bridge. Donny carried a picnic basket and wore a sailor suit because, as he explained, he was a second-generation Navy veteran who always observed Memorial Day.

With large, rusty plates covering holes in the pedestrian walkway, the bridge had become a rotting hazard since the time of Sonny Rollins. Lacking the refinement of the Manhattan Bridge, and without the heraldry of the Brooklyn or the 59th Street bridges, the Williamsburg bridge had the regal splendor of a broken erector set. Tuli Kufperberg once told me that he was the mysterious person Allen Ginsberg mentions in "Howl" as having survived jumping off the Brooklyn Bridge, only to pause, as if reliving the sorry incident, and solemnly conclude, "I'm glad it wasn't the Williamsburg Bridge. No one would have cared." And yet, there I was.

About halfway up, where the bridge levels off, Donny turned to reveal a spectacular view of Manhattan. He then suggested that we make camp there in celebration of the holiday. Lisa reached into the basket and pulled out a few bottles of Thunderbird. I was given a bottle and, using the view of the city as a map, Donny started yapping about where to go and what to do in time of (imminent) apocalypse.

Before long, Donny and Lisa exchanged whispers and the usual oral scene ensued. By this time, I was getting accustomed to it, and stared into the skyline as we chatted so as to ignore the obvious. As per always, Donny punctuated the episode with a knee-buckling set of spasms so extreme that one could speculate that they were embellished for my benefit. Returning, then, to the wine, he graciously offered Lisa, or himself, to me, "unless there's anything I can help you with."

After declining these overtures, we resumed losing the evening in Thunderbird-infused fantasies about post-apocalyptic survival without electricity, phone, police, fire fighters, or hospitals. After a time, we came to realize that we'd missed the show.

Turning back to Manhattan, the city lights doubled and spun slowly, like in a kaleidoscope. I told Donny that I was too drunk to go home to grandma's. He and Lisa exchanged whispers, "You can crash with us, but you'll have to sleep in our bed." Probing the situation, I asked, "Could I just sleep on your couch?" Donny was adamant, "No. You'll be our guest, and as a guest, you'll respect the rules of the house."

Louis's prediction weighed on me, and I declined with words rendered blunt from booze. A virgin in all respects, I had no desire to receive carnal knowledge from Lisa, or Donny, for that matter. About a half block later, I slumped into the doorway of an abandoned fire station on Broome Street. Sliding down, considering a nap, I took off my glasses, which drew the world into microscopic focus. Compared with the ocean depths, the sidewalk sports an ecosystem yet I didn't see the spider. I wondered if it had died or got bored and wandered off or if it was hiding from me. We all know that spider webs don't make themselves. Leaning over, I buried that microverse in a cascade of vomit. Getting up, I walked the night, resolving to put some distance between me and my would-be mentor, and slipped back to grandma's in the early morning, passing out hard.

***

The next time I saw Lisa was in front of CBGB. She

walked up looking a bit down, wearing a skinhead bomber jacket and doc martens, and opened her arms for a hug: "Did you hear what happened to Donny?"

"No."

"He had it coming to him."

"What?"

"I came home one day to find Donny in the bathtub with my kids."

I looked at her, unsure what she was getting at.

"He promised that he would never touch my kids."

The long and short of it was that Donny had molested Lisa's kids and she told her friends in the skinhead community, who were more than willing to teach him the cost of bad parentage.

After that, I didn't see Donny for a few years. When we next ran into one another, in the backyard of ABCNORIO around 1992, he was long-since healed, but his face was a bit crooked. We were cordial, but I was no longer interested in his friendship. Donny died from complications associated with AIDS in 1996.

You'll Always Be an Asshole

My teeth chattered between snatches of provolone as I considered my options from inside the walk-in freezer. Absent-mindedly clutching a mop, I reflected on my "career path." Since college, I'd already been a security guard, which had the dry-gagging odor of stale cigarettes and dead flies about it, and I still recall hanging off a hand truck at the opposite end of a filing cabinet at an ill-fated furniture moving gig. Oh, and for a time I was a community organizer for SANE: The Committee for a Sane Nuclear Policy, a radical organization that banked on fear of nuclear holocaust.

Stepping out of the refrigerator, I shuffled back up to the front counter. Ken shot me the stinkeye as he passed, "Tag, you're it. And I want to hear you this time."

Projecting my voice for Ken's sake, I approached the register robotically reciting "Welcome to Frank's Subs. How.... may I... help... you?"

Don't get me wrong; Ken wasn't a bad kid, but I wasn't going to go full-on belly up for $3.75 an hour—then the wages of my liberal arts education. Before you object to my use of the word "kid," mind you: he was still in high school. For a more complete picture, imagine him a pimply eighteen, pale, maybe a bit Irish, with a plumber's butt, in an apron.

As I made a dozen or more roast beef or Italian subs, I reflected on how I came to work at Big Frank's. One night, coming home sore and bruised from the furniture moving gig, my eyes set upon a "help wanted sign" at a franchise location around the block from where I was living. I made a fast arrangement. I wore my only tie—a skinny black tie—and my only button-down white shirt to the interview. The hiring manager was a super-fat white guy. His office had fake wood paneling on its walls and behind him hung an extra-wide horizontal photo of an obese, greasy, Italian-looking meatball—Big Frank himself—standing behind a table with a six-foot submarine sandwich on it.

Pausing over my resume, he intoned, as if to welcome me into an ancient fraternal order: "A college graduate? You could have a big future at Big Frank's. How does that sound?"

"It sounds good, sir." It sounded like a complete horrorshow. I didn't even eat meat.

"Good, that's what we like to hear at Big Frank's." Over the course of two or three cigarettes, he regaled me with tales of his thirty-year odyssey to submarine sandwich supremacy, the details of which I have, mercifully, long since suppressed. "Like I said, you could have a big future at Big Frank's, but there is a catch."

"A catch?"

Riffing on his cigarette and pausing to enjoy it, he nodded his head and explained: "Like me, you're going to have to work your way up in the company from the lowest position. It's the only way that you can fully understand our system."

So, there I was, making study of the Big Frank's "system," one sub at a time, when I decided to toss my career to the fates by joining the pool of temporary office workers. By wearing the apron, I'd already given up sovereignty over my appearance, so an office uniform was merely an equivalent level of domination. A Marxist of sorts, I'd have to resist fancying myself petit bourgeois, the loss of class-consciousness being a constant temptation, but $3.75 an hour was leaving me hungry and working under Ken's iron sneaker was not making me happy. The notion of a thirty-year long march from custodial duties to over-stuffed sandwich superstardom set a planetoid of molten acid cheese, a remnant of a slice I'd wolfed down on my way over, adrift from my stomach, up through my esophagus, and into my mouth.

Our heavyset Sherlock Holmes returned from his fact-finding mission to the frozen tundra: "There are three less slices of provolone in the fridge than I cut this morning. How did that happen?"

Ken was just doing his job, but I was no longer willing to play along. "Must be those mice again."

"Those mice are going to have to pay for a whole sandwich."

"Fine, and they can take the rest of my shift." And I proceeded to remove my apron.

"Your shift is over in five minutes."

Taking off my cap and apron, I squeaked in defiance and left. I was trying to be a snotty punk revolutionary. Quitting at the end of my shift and imitating a mouse came off as light fare. I resolved to do better in the future.

***

That night, I dashed off an abridged version of my resume to a few agencies that place temporary workers. After a week or thereabouts, I received a call. Someone asked if I understood computers.

"Sure, what do you mean?"

"Do you know Fortran?"

"Fortran, the business language? It's my favorite—I practically majored in it." Actually, all I knew about Fortran was that it had business applications. I was too busy studying the opinions of my professors about The Vendee, among random aspects of the French Revolution, to learn a practical skill, like computer science. I was given the location of the company and I reported on time the next day. I turned the computer on. It had an interface that I could not understand. I'm not the best at bluffing. They had me out the door before lunch, but I got a full-day's pay.

After a few weeks, I received an offer from a different temp agency: "Do you have any experience in auditing?"

"Auditing? Yes, oh, yes, lots of auditing." For the princely sum of $4.25 an hour I was hired to comb through reels of microfilm cataloguing land owned by the State of New York. Compared to other jobs I'd had, it offered a pedestrian paradise—no physical labor, no meat, no ideological head trips, a modest raise in wages, and it was work that I actually could do. Fascinating? Expressive? Redemptive in terms of class struggle? Well, no, but not bad. And besides, when I told people that I was an "auditor," it pinned their ears back.

During the first few months, I worked in an old office behind a stairwell at a desk completely hidden from view and I worked hard. About once a week, Lauren or Ray—the supervisors—would check on me, occasionally muttering something about my outperforming the rest of my cohort.

Shortly after that, I was pulled into a large room and assigned a desk. All of the workers hired by this agency were now combined into a room seating about thirty. We were an odd lot of working-class people: black, white, Latin, and, with my moustache that didn't connect in the middle, I was still punky.

An (attempted) adjustment to society.

In the back, behind a row of opaque plastic windows, was an office where all four of the supervisors had their desks. A few times each day, at varied intervals, a supervisor would pop out to observe that we were all present and productive. Sometimes we'd be lectured on the evils of talking to one another, which is what it seemed like they were doing whenever the door was closed. We heard them chattering like the adults in a Peanuts cartoon. Without recognizing what they were saying, it was clear to those of us voicing whispered opinions that their conversations had a cadence and volubility that scarcely accompanies serious shoptalk.

"He'll never get her."

"What?"

"She'll never go for Ray—he's not her type." Sitting in front of me was Ralph, a straggly little white guy, in his mid-30s, with bad hair, bad skin, and bad posture, who stank of cigarettes and never took off his winter coat. Even when he wore cologne, Ralph had the scent of "skell" all around him, as evidenced by his ability to toss his voice backwards through his head without turning—the sort of skill someone might develop if they'd ever lived under supervision. I asked him what he thought our betters did behind closed doors: "Ray's on his knees begging for the ice queen to melt, and if she's already on her knees with someone else, then Ray's down on his elbows." In installments offered over the next few days, my neighbor shared what seemed like a shrewd microanalysis of Ray's unrequited lust for Lauren.

Across the following few weeks, Ralph emptied his pockets of the vast trove of wisdom he'd collected across his craggy life, including such vital nuggets as the proper etiquette for entering gang territory, how to check if hookers have herpes or if they're cops, never admitting anything to police, and how to quickly test the quality of coke, junk, and crack. Scooping it all up, I could have received a certificate in Lumpen Prole Studies.

One day, we returned from lunch to find official memos on everyone's desk approximating the following:

```
                    MEMO

TO: Everyone
Date: 8/??/8?
FROM: Ray
RE: Break Policy

 Employees are taking too many Breaks,
which is interfering with productivity.
In the name of fairness and efficiency,
we will observe the following Break
Policy without exception.
 Employees must take a 15-minute
Break at 10:15am; a lunch from 12:00
to 12:30pm, either outside or at
their desks; and a 15-minute Break at
2:15pm. Employees may take Breaks at
their desks.
 All other breaks will require the
approval of a Supervisor, as under
New York State Employment Code.
```

As the door to the back office was open, my fellow workers quietly exchanged gestures of displeasure.

Ray stepped out from the inner office into the center of the shared outer room in full, blow-dried glory. Lauren and the other two managers stood in the back scanning our reactions for signs of resistance. Placing his hand beside his ear, Ray asked, "Has everyone thought about the new policies?" Folks awkwardly, but minimally, made sounds of compliance. Putting his hands on his hips, he looked back at Lauren, as if to ask her, "Does anyone have any questions?" Then Ray stared into each of our faces, one by one, meeting our eyes, peering into the backs of our brains for signs of resistance. Satisfied with what he saw, he sauntered out of the room. We heard some cheerful chatter inside the back office—the sound of success.

Ralph's throaty little ventriloquist whisper issued comment out of the back of his head: "Ray thinks that this will get his dick wet."

"What are you going to do?"

"Have a smoke," Ralph darted out the door.

"But..." It was 4:12 in the afternoon—not a designated "Break" time.

Ray and Lauren emerged from the back office together wearing their winter coats. They crossed to the front of the office in tandem, lost in an inside joke, until Lauren pointed to Ralph's empty desk.

Conferring busily, the two returned to the back office, closing the door with punctuation. Ray soon darted out, and paced back and forth across the center of the room.

When Ralph returned to the office, Ray stepped in front of his desk: "You read the new policy. You needed to ask my permission. Where were you?"

"Outside."

"What were you doing there?"

"Thinking about the new policy."

Everyone laughed.

"That's it. You're fired. You're out. You need to leave now. I've already called the agency and now I will call security. You only have a few minutes or you're going to be arrested." Walking over to a phone, he pointed to the doorway and commanded: "Go!"

Ralph walked toward the door, and then turned: "Sure, Ray, you can fire me, and guess what? I'll find another job, but you'll always be an asshole."

***

We returned to work the next day still sore from the beating we'd witnessed. As he had the day before, Ray asked if we understood the policy and that there were no exceptions to it. When the door to the back office closed, the choir of gestures from my fellow proles was noticeably grimmer—sadly resigned—than before. During lunch, a few coworkers openly considering quitting, but everyone needed the cash.

That evening, I took action. I asked a friend to type the following, which I photocopied onto the official stationery that Ray had used. The following day, I took lunch at my desk and, once the office was empty, put it on everyone's desk, including those in the back office:

```
                  MEMO
TO: Everyone
Date: 8/??/8?
FROM: Ray
RE: Bathroom Break Policy


 Employees    are    taking    too    many
Bathroom Breaks, which is interfering
with productivity.   In the name of
fairness    and   efficiency,    we    will
observe the following Bathroom Break
Policy without exception.
 Employees   must   take   a   5-minute
Bathroom Break at 10:45am and at
2:45pm, and must take a 10-minute
Bathroom Break at 1:00pm. Employees
may not take Bathroom Breaks at their
desks.
 If an employee has not left the
stall after 10-minutes, the toilet
```

paper will contract into the wall, the toilet will flush, a siren will sound, and the stall door will open. Violators will be prosecuted to the fullest extent of New York State Bathroom Code.

Any additional Bathroom Breaks or anticipated Bathroom Break Extensions require the approval of a Supervisor.

My coworkers were the first to shuffle back from break, arriving in small solemn groups. On reading my memo, I heard people say that this was their final straw. An older black lady complained of having a weak bladder. I wanted to reassure them that this was a joke, but felt like I needed to hang back to play this through to the end. Next, three of the managers returned without Ray.

About an hour before quitting time, Ray swaggered into the office with the subtlety of Fred Flintstone arriving home from work. Lauren rushed from the back office to greet him: "Ray, I never knew you had such a great sense of humor!" Ray smiled awkwardly, accepting the unexpected compliment, but soon indicated that he didn't understand what she was driving at. They walked to the back office, whose door slammed shut. A few beats later, Ray stomped into the center of our tiny town square, his officemates looking on in support from the back, and, red-faced, demanded to know who wrote the new memo. I pondered my options. On the one hand, I could quietly continue to work there as a cowardly petit bourgeois, or I could step out into history to avenge Ralph, my fellow proletarian, in a blaze of self-righteous glory.

"I wrote the memo."

Ray's beet-red face cracked into a taught smile:

"You're fired. Collect your things."

Summoning the loserish pride of Al Pacino in *Dog Day Afternoon*, I met his eyes: "Look around, in the weeks to come, everyone here will tell you the same thing: 'You can fire me, and guess what? I'll find another job, but you will always be an asshole.'"

Who Wants Some?

In the summer of 1990, I lived with my grandma and prepared for graduate study at The New School, once a haven for scholars fleeing Fascism.

On the day at play, I fed on Platonism in NYU's Bobst Library. After library closing, in the early evening, several hardcovers filling out my knapsack, I dropped over to Downtown Beirut, a little bar on First Avenue with an assortment of melancholic punk songs—like "I Believe" by The Buzzcocks—on its jukebox. To take the edge off a sticky night, the sort of night when even close friends can become enemies and true enemies take no prisoners, I sipped a cold American beer. One watery beer.

Resuming my walk home, I idled at Tompkins Square Park, which hosted "speak outs" against the first Gulf War. I'd long been charmed by New York's Hyde Park, witnessing, over the years, the fulminations of John the Communist, Allen Ginsberg, Frances Goldin, Roger Manning, Eric Drooker, Pete Missing, and a hundred million other would-be seers and saviors.

There were about fifty or more radicals, community organizers, and fellow travelers at Tompkins that night. Notably, the Revolutionary Communist Party was on hand. Burning American flags, the R.C.P.'s hallmark, was real upsetting for some folks back then. At least ten cops were monitoring the goings-on.

Two large white guys emerged from Alcatraz, a tough-guy faux-biker bar then on Avenue A and St. Marks Place. Crossing the street, they wrestled with the crowd of leftists, trying to scrum their way in to rescue the flag. The crowd pushed back. Exhausted from the heat and burdened with library books, I observed the scuffle, motionless and silent.

Rebuffed from the flag, the larger of the two counter-protestors, square-jawed and sporting a goatee and earrings which gave him the wild menace of a pirate, challenged anyone and everyone to a fight. Rhythmically raising and lowering his fists, he bellowed: "Who wants some? Who wants some?"

Approaching, he lowered his pirate head somewhat to meet my eyes: "Do you want some?" Deep in mind, detached, surveying life on this planet as if transmitting information to another dimension, I was still, a mere spectator. Then my head exploded, and my glasses burst into the air. (Witnesses later told me that he had given me a headbutt. I certainly hadn't seen it coming.)

Reassembling my face and scanning the sidewalk for my glasses, "Jerry the Peddler," one of the protestors, asked whether I wanted to press charges. I told him that I did. Having already broken several bones in life, I knew that my nose was fucked, but I was too pissed to seek medical attention just then. We walked over to the police across the street, who'd surely seen the entire event unfold.

"He wants to press charges," Jerry told the cops.

A cop came forward, "Let me ask him myself. What do you want to do?"

Stepping forward, I told him: "I want to press charges."

"Are you sure?"

"I'm sure."

"Are you sure that you're sure? We're always asked to take people in and then the charges get dropped. Do you want to waste my time?" Cynicism ran deep.

I insisted, "Yes, I will press charges, but I don't want him to get a good look at me. After all, he slugged me in front of fifty of my best friends and a dozen cops."

The cop reassured me, "Don't worry, they will

process him in the holding cells in the back. And then bring him down to 'The Tombs.' He won't be out for 24 hours. Are YOU SURE that YOU want to go through with this?"

"I'm sure." I was sure. I really was.

Turning his eyes to the sky, the cop turned and motioned to two others, and the three of them went into Alcatraz. They soon fished out the big guy, leading him in cuffs into a car. The cop I'd spoken with told me to follow him and get into his car.

After a short drive to the precinct house, I saw that the other car was already there. I entered the main room of the precinct with my officer, who quickly left me, telling me to wait for him. The only other person in the room, seated and handcuffed to his chair, and chafing like Hannibal Lechter on a diet, was my attacker, the oversized pirate, whose maniac eyes reached toward me. I turned to hide my face and quickly ducked into an empty office, where I sat down behind a desk, put my feet up like Bugs Bunny, and closed the door. Not long after, a police officer entered, exchanged seats with me, and took my deposition.

Grandma was watching TV with my great aunt when I came home. Greatly consumed with *Murder, She Wrote* (her favorite!), she absent-mindedly inquired: "*Nu? So, votz cookin'?*" Darting quickly down the hall, I announced that I was hot, tired, taking a shower, and then retiring early. Fortunately, she was too dazzled by Angela Lansbury to examine me. Like my great aunt, grandma was fascinated with grisly depictions of violence on television, but emotionally ill-equipped to deal with the real thing. Staring back from the bathroom mirror, bloodshot eyes winced back from a face blossoming black and purple, with a dark red line demarcating my nose like Korea.

After grandma went out that morning, I dragged my sore ass to a neighborhood "hospital." Without a doctor on-call on Sundays, it was more a place where damaged people congregated than a functioning medical facility. After a few hours, my number was called. Arching his eyebrows, a little Puerto Rican guy asked me what was wrong. I gave him an abridged version of the preceding. Screwing up his face into a ball, he offered a possible diagnosis: "You might have meningitis; an infection of your brain from your broken nose. I'm not a doctor, but I do have access to an X-ray machine. We can take a look." He X-rayed my head.

That night, I somehow eluded grandma who, come to think of it, was, by this stage of life, a bit out-to-sea and easily distracted. The next day, I called into my job as a statistician for the Board of Education, and set out for Beth Israel, the hospital which had stolen me from the womb in the first place.

After an hour or two in the waiting room, I finally met with a medical intern, digesting the story—the war, the flag, a pirate, my head, cops, my nose, Hannibal, my eyes, an x-ray of my head, and meningitis, with an emphasis on the lattermost. Up my nose with a little flashlight, the intern floated: "Have you ever thought about rhinoplasty?"

I stared back blankly, unsure what he was on about.

"Rhinoplasty, you know, a nosejob?"

A psychopathic pirate had given me a brain infection, and here was some wet-eared medical student telling me what he thought of my face (not much). Directing him back to my neurosis: "Yeah, I know what rhinoplasty is. What about the meningitis?"

Sighing just slightly, he continued, "You probably don't have meningitis, but if you'd ever considered rhinoplasty, this would be the perfect time. The break is clean and well-placed. It just needs to be reset. If, of course, you don't want to, your nose will heal much the way it looked before the incident. Your choice."

Oy vey. An overwrought fear of brain infection had brought me to face-to-face with deciding whether I'd have my nose "fixed" to meet dominant cultural norms or continue to stand nose-to-nose, with my people. My nose, visible sign of my peoplehood, points down toward its hidden analogue in my trousers. As one surgery had made me a Jew from the waist on down, signing an intimate covenant, another could undo it from the waist up and in public. Generations of forebears trapped in the genetic isolation of villages across what my grandfather called "Russia-Poland" had forged my almost stereotypical Jewface, and now, in a flash of modern plasticity, I was invited to undo it. After all, my parents knew that it was important to not be too conspicuous: they gave me an American first name, dressed my brother and I like the non-Jewish kids, sent us to public school, and were careful to avoid giving me a middle name beginning with the letter "E."

One great-uncle, under a false floor, nervously hid from Cossacks, holding his breath, while many were not so lucky. I see them stomped by villagers and soldiers and exterminators; sentenced and tortured by people of nobility and men of The Cloth; stuffed away into barns lit aflame; forbidden to be seen in the village square on a Sunday under punishment of stoning; on a hill with a man nailed to a cross behind maybe six million Jews nailed to crosses, and pulling out a bit further, an ocean of all sorts of people abused, and otherwise brutalized, extending around this world several times and out into space, as much a sign of intelligent life as a ring of orbiting space junk. In a sharp second, I dismissed surgery.

A week or so later, I received a call from the local district attorney, who sympathetically took notes as I recounted the attack and its implications for my civil liberties. She asked me if I was speaking or holding a sign when the attack occurred. No to both: "Well, this is not a violation of your civil liberties, but it is a clear case of assault and battery. His only defense is that his brother is serving abroad, and he feels strongly about the war. Although you don't need to come in, it would *really* help the case. He's a law student at N.Y.U. If we can make the charges 'stick,' this could keep him from practicing law."

Reflecting on my attacker's brazenness, as well as his size, the unwillingness of the police to get involved, and the sometimes appalling failures of our judicial system, I envisioned him at the door to grandma's apartment, which was often unlocked, as my grandma and great aunt constantly went back and forth across the hall between their apartments.

As push almost came to shove, I *did* press charges, though I refused to testify in person, so my attacker was assigned community service, which, I was disappointed to learn, he never performed.

And my nose? It's as bent as it was before, no more and no less.

I Was a Teenage Marxist
(or The Importance of Following Baseball)

"Are you right-hand dominant?" It was the second time I'd faced that dismal question in a just few months, and both times my answer was met with condolences. "Ah, I see." The doctor shook his head solemnly.

My hand lay limp, a hairy tentacle grafted onto my arm in some failed genetic experiment, more like "E.T." than anything recognizably human. Its ring finger was held together at an awkward angle by a tangle of steel rods looking like a wayward erector set. When the doctor showed it to me, I grimly turned to my mom and introduced her to my "Frankenfinger."

"An immobilized inner finger will prevent you from making a fist, which is important for grasping things, or just about any practical use of this hand." As it was explained, my right hand would be virtually useless, but there was a solution. "Actually," the doctor confided, "when I was a teenager, I had a similar injury. Fortunately, a doctor was able to remove the finger and now I have complete use of my hand." He displayed his hand, which was, indeed, missing the very same finger and was now, as he made a fist, demonstrably useable.

Our "right hands" have been symbolic of meaningful engagement with the world for millennia, which was what I was after in the first place. While I'd never seen what an actual politically ascendant left-wing movement looked like, I'd already quaffed deeply of ideology in punkland, and while working for Democratic Socialists of America (through which I met Bernie Sanders) and SANE (where I met Abbie Hoffman). Capping it off, I was then a graduate student at The New School editing an academic journal informed by the Critical Theory of The Frankfurt School. Classes never referenced Soviet purges, China's "Cultural Revolution," or the "killing fields" of Cambodia. No "café communist," the alchemy of theory called, so it seemed, for a dose of *praxis*—direct action—to make it real.

***

To tap into the symbolic resonance of American traditions when the press arrived, banners were painted with themes of Independence Day: "liberty," "freedom," and "justice." We knew that the cops would be dispatched away from their posts by the squats on 13th Street for crowd control at the official celebrations—the fireworks—which would give us the opportunity to hang the banners from the windows of the vacated squat and wait for them. Then, the true fireworks would begin, in front of the press, framed with carefully crafted language.

At the appointed hour, the padlocks keeping the squat closed were snapped and banners were hung. As the police tried to regain entry, those inside threw detritus out of its windows, and a sympathetic crowd gathered out in the street. I mixed in. I could see the police forcibly remove one of the anarchists and hit him—a golden opportunity for the righteous indignation that I craved. At the time, in the mid-1990s, 40-ounce malt liquors were the drink choice of neighborhood degenerates and there were plenty of empty bottles on the street. I picked one up and threw it, a glass football, in a perfect spiral exploding on the sidewalk a few feet in front of the police, right in their faces.

Unfortunately, they saw me do it. After a brief deliberation, they charged at me. At first, I didn't realize that I'd been fingered. It happened quickly. Four or five cops soon came upon me like a wave. The particulars elude recall, but it seems I spun like a pinwheel and was soon splayed out on my back in the gutter with them kicking me. A hand reached down in front of my face. Grabbing it, I was brought up to my feet. Asking for my glasses, which had gone flying in the turbulence, I heard one say: "there they are." Next heard was the crunch of a shoe stamping on them. The rest of my experience was seen by profoundly myopic eyes.

I was taken to a police car. I could see a sympathetic crowd watching and I thought about raising my fist in rebellion, but my head was soon pushed down into the car. This photo was taken.

Assuming the position.

At the precinct house, I was placed in a holding pen. Over the next few hours, many others were brought in from the action for processing. When it was my turn to be fingerprinted, I showed the printer my finger. Excusing himself from touching it, he called for the arresting officer—a blond, muscular white guy with long hair, the sort whose fellow cops might call a "cowboy"—to process me. The other officers and many of the other people in custody watched as I extended my grotesquely distended appendage. As if to imply that I was already broken before my rough arrest, and to ridicule me, the cop played to his audience, chortling "He's got a deformed digit." A few cops nervously laughed along. I told him that I needed medical attention, and for the next several hours, long after the others had already been brought to central booking, I was repeatedly told that I "would receive medical attention."

At dawn, I was placed in a van and brought to Bellevue, New York City's main public hospital. As there were no bed vacancies, the cops held a tarp in front of me in the hospital lobby. I was told to change into a hospital gown and put my clothes, watch, shoes, and wallet in a bag. Then I laid down as I was handcuffed to a gurney. I asked about my clothes and was assured that they would "follow" me. The officer assigned now to me, a black woman, told me that I needed to be on good behavior, or she would twist my finger. Putting her face in front of mine to press her point into my head, she glibly declared, brain-to-brain, that she knew how to hurt me. I was struck by her sincerity.

I laid still and silent on the bed, closing my eyes. Another gurney was placed beside mine and I heard an orderly mutter the words "infectious disease" before disappearing. I motioned to my officer and told her. She left to inquire and, before long, returned to tell me that a bed was now available. The trip upstairs was chaotic, with her slamming the gurney into hospital walls. "Since," she explained, "the bed has no brakes," she couldn't be expected to drive it safely.

The room had four beds, three of which were populated by other men, all of whom had large tubes reaching from their bowels to buckets collecting their bile. This much I could make out, even with my myopia, which, mercifully, obscured grisly plumbing details. None spoke English. For the next two days, the only people I could hope to communicate with were the police assigned to me. I was handcuffed to the bed and my other arm was attached to an I.V. As a hospital is not a "secure area," I was denied a phone call. Every time the police switched, they showed my file to the next cop. To engage my captors, I deployed knowledge of baseball factoids gained largely second-hand from an apartment mate, though many declined my entreaties. (I neurotically continue to superstitiously monitor baseball stats in case I need to be "relatable" if incarcerated again.)

An orderly examined my finger, asking "Are you right-hand dominant?" When I confirmed, he sighed, "you may lose the use of your hand," and, before I had time to respond, he melted back into the smudge of images. I requested to use the bathroom, but it was denied because I "could not be left alone" and "a hospital is not a 'secure area.'" I was ankle-cuffed to the bed, my handcuff was released, and I was given a bedpan to relieve myself. When I was done, the process was reversed each time I had to "go," which was not often, and I didn't poop for the duration of the affair. Nearly blind, isolated, and affixed to a bed, I contemplated surgery and arraignment.

In the early morning of day two, I was leg-cuffed to a gurney. An officer beside me, I was wheeled into surgery. The leg-cuff would remain throughout the performance, as, it was explained, prisoners had been known to try to "make a break for it" during an operation. A little curtain was placed beside my hand on a tray to spare me the ghoulish action. My right hand was placed on the cool page of an open textbook which soothed the back of my hand. The surgeons, who were medical students, conferred. Puzzled by the odd configuration of bones, one conjectured, "I think it goes like this." The other differed: "No, look at the photo, it goes like that." (Looking at it just now, I wonder if the first one may have been right.) Awaking in my hospital room, stirred by a cop, I was informed that I'd be brought to central booking for arraignment. It stung when I tried to open my eyes, which began to tear up. Blinded, I asked if I could go to the bathroom to clean my face. Instead, I was leg-cuffed and offered a basin of water at bedside. The water felt cool and refreshing. My eyes reopened.

I asked for my clothes and was told that the bag with my stuff couldn't be found. I had no clothing, no glasses, no ID, and no one knew where I was. Envisioning a *Village Voice* cover titled "The Naked Civil Offender," I considered going to jail in a hospital gown. Reflecting on the unwanted attention I might have attracted, I demanded to speak with the Patient Advocate. After some to do, I was given oversized green prison pants, which I held up with hands cuffed behind me, and placed in a van.

As a medical prisoner, I was granted a separate cell at "The Tombs" of central booking. Now in jail, I was finally allowed to call a friend and assigned a public defender. Taken to a courtroom, I was seated on a bench with random miscreants awaiting arraignment. Just before my case, the presiding judge's shift ended—it was midnight of day two—and all the prisoners were dumped in a room together. My eyes were met by those of a tall, slim, dark-eyed black guy about my age with a leg in a cast, who motioned for me to sit beside him. With the door closed, folks exchanged stories candidly, none claiming wrongful accusation. My instant friend opened up, half-bragging and half-complaining: "I'm from Harlem, where I'm well known. You see, I snatched this lady's gold necklace and ran, but they ran after me and gave [me] a beating." Sharing that I'd been picked up for fighting the cops, there was general approbation, but the story that really animated the group was told by two sisters who had been working in a crack house in The Bronx when it was raided. When one proudly announced, "I swallowed a bag of crack vials," I winced at the medical risks of having little glass bottles inside her and how hard it would be to pass them, but this fungible commodity brought instant celebrity. One woman offered: "My sister is in Riker's [Island]—you've gotta look her up when you get there!" I was summarily charged with three felonies (rioting, resisting arrest, and assault), as well as two misdemeanors (disorderly conduct and reckless endangerment), and released to my own recognizance.

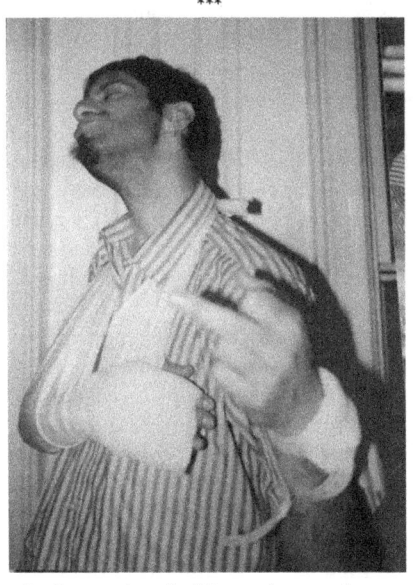

***

It takes a nation of millions to keep me down.

After six months of physical therapy, my finger and its hand remained lame. After the first surgeon proposed removing my finger, root-and-stem, I sought a second opinion. The second surgeon, who struck me as arrogant, believed that he could fix it. I was doubtful, but game. During the procedure, he ordered me to move my finger and I told him that I couldn't. He forcefully repeated the command: "You can move your finger now. Move it!" I tried to but couldn't see it without my glasses. Agitated, he put my hand directly in front of my face and repeated. I saw it move and wept as if I'd seen a Divine Act. After a few more months of physical therapy, my finger gained mobility and my hand regained strength.

***

On the assigned date, I reported to court, and a few minutes before I was to go before a judge, my public defender arrived and swept me aside. I excitedly pointed out that the written complaint alleged that I threw rocks at the police, which was untrue, as I'd thrown a bottle. When I told him that, since their deposition was incorrect, I'd been attacked and held in violation of my civil liberties, he grew stern: "No, you attacked the police and what you got was 'street justice.' If you fight this, you will lose and serve time. Is that what you want? Admit your guilt and let me ask for a plea bargain."

I needed legal advice to help me with my legal advice. In high school, I'd been arrested for paltry possession of a contraband vegetable. During probation, a daytrip to the Fishkill Correctional Facility brought insight into what awaited me if I continued. We talked in a circle and met in small groups with ACTUAL "lifers," people serving life sentences. Umar, a very broad and fit lifer I'd been assigned to, approached the large group: "Suppose you are new or brought into a new facility, and someone walks up and offers you a cigarette. Do you take it?" The answer was clearly "no," but no one knew why. "Nothing is free. [They're] gonna collect later and you may not like the price. Every time you come into a new house, you're going to have to fight, no matter who you are—everybody." Umar asked a large, blonde kid to stand up. "In your 'hood, I bet you're a bad ass." The kid smiled big and proud, laughing to his pals. "But in the Big House, you're Farrah Fawcett." His face drawing into a frown, the kid was told to sit down. Umar then told us about a white kid who was brought to Fishkill: "He wasn't ready when a bunch of brothers got him in the shower. They shoved a newspaper in his mouth to keep him from screaming while they ran a train on him. He choked to death." My choice was simple and had to be made immediately: I agreed to the plea bargain.

***

After about a year, the whole affair ran its legal and medical courses. At the end of the day, I was charged with a "moving violation" and my finger was disfigured, but functional. I'd reached out, wanting to leave a meaningful mark on "the world" in the name of "justice," and instead, the only marks were on me and my "Frankenfinger."

Since then, I've come to the subtle intuition that I'm not, somehow, cut out to use my right hand for acts of violence, regardless of how presumably noble they may appear in the heat of a mess. Perhaps, dear reader, if there is some discernible teleology to it all, I've been fated to use my right hand to write this for you to read. Now achieved, is my life without further purpose?

Requiem for a Tenor: The Life and Death of Jack Terricloth

On Wednesday, May 12, 2021, Peter Ventantonio, known to the civilized world as "Jack Terricloth," died in his little Brooklyn grotto, alone, of the delirium tremens. It was thirty years, perhaps even to the very day, from when he stepped into my life. Flashing back to that day, I can still envision him bopping into Reconstruction Records (a punk record shop in New York City where I worked) and wandering into the back of the store. Like a character from *La Novelle Vague*, he was bold, yet refined and reserved, an actor in search of a new movie to live in.

Peter was living on-and-off with his folks, and fronting Sticks and Stones, a punk band offering cynical and snotty rebellion against the liberal upper-middle class milieu of his central New Jersey homeland: a "Theme Song for Nothing." As his father was a successful and dapper lawyer, judge, and Democratic Party nominee for mayor of his hometown, punk nihilism was, for him, the most available route to teenage individuation.

Peter was sick—*sick!*—of New Jersey and had come to New York City as an ambitious young man hungry to find inspiration and promethean self-creation in the downtown New York cultural underground. Soon after, I helped Peter get his first NYC apartment in my old building at 620-622 East 11th Street. He lived there for two years, sharing 425 square feet of genuine Lower East Side tenement squalor with Osamu (aka Sam) Kawahara, a high school friend who also took up bass duties in Sticks and Stones. Peter and I would sometimes climb the stairs to the roof of the building with a few bottles of wine. I'd exchange notes on the Weimar Republic (then the subject of my studies at The New School) for his insights into the gothic sensibility, including the virtues of nocturnal living. (He even made me a mixed tape titled "Intro to Goth" in playful parody of my studies.) By bringing goth into my life, Peter liberated me from didacticism and reignited my interest in art as a refuge from reality. (I'd had a passing dalliance with horror punk in the 1980s which was eclipsed by politics.) By the end of the night, we'd howl up into the deep inky still of the starless Manhattan sky. To those on the street and to sleepless neighbors, it must've sounded like a little lost wolfpack up there.

Though then in the twilight of youth, Peter already had an ethic of sorts, and people were invited into his life along axes of common interest: he liked wine and liquor, pre-war and pre-TV culture and style (he'd grab my tie and say "we are little gentlemen"), meat, and, sadly, cocaine (a big-league taboo nostalgic to the 1920s and certainly non-fattening). Conversely, he was against drinking beer (deeming it fattening and undignified), heavy metal and grunge (along with guitar solos and long hair), sunlight (he told me to "stick to the shady side of the street"), marijuana and LSD (like many things hippie), and veganism (partially also because of its hippie connotations). And he didn't like to brush his tiny teeth (which turned purple when he drank wine) or wear underwear (some borders he simply would not abide), which, at least, were things he never expected of a friend. Without doubt, some found Peter to be pretentious, and, indeed, he was bored of official reality. In this life we either wear uniforms or costumes.

Around this time, in addition to a long-term relationship, Peter had a dalliance with a woman who lived with an enormous python. And, yes, the snake twined between them as they performed acts of carnal delight. At the time, a profound allergy to cats put a damper on his more serious relationship, ending when his partner chose feline intimacy over his. Although abundantly charming and continuously flirtatious, Peter lived largely as a serial monogamist, and most of his girlfriends eventually left him for one reason or another. One eloped with a friend, which launched his first deep dive into the bottle, and another stole from him. That old cliché about "love and war" sometimes rings too true.

Peter first found steady employ as a switchboard operator at The Metropolitan Museum of Art, and, later, as bartender at The Continental, a club on 3rd Avenue around the corner from St. Marks Place with live punky music every night. Rather than inspiring him to rock out, watching a non-stop stream of cranked-up tattooed rebels cheapened its appeal. After all, this was the early to mid-1990s, and, thanks to Nirvana, noisy rock music was becoming ubiquitous in popular culture—opening sporting events and scoring commercials. Peter wanted to find an aesthetic of his own.

Once, while gallivanting about in Tompkins Square Park, Peter was nervously approached by Whitey Sterling, vocalist of The Stiffs, a musical outfit crossing punk with a vaguely Victorian sensibility. The Stiffs' original drummer had jumped ship and they offered Peter a turn in the hot seat. He declined, summarily informing them that he was a singer, not a drummer.

At the time, Whitey worked at The Wandering Dragon Trading Company, a shop on 10th Street thick with a mysterious ambience of taxidermy, medical oddities in formaldehyde, old maps, and bizarro bric-a-brac from the Freemasons and their ilk. The proprietor, Adrian Gilboe, was an antiquarian well-versed in pre-war European culture and an alcoholic. Adrian joined Peter as a bartender at The Continental, where he introduced Peter to the circus creep of Brecht and Weil's Threepenny Opera. In its opening number, "Mack, the Knife," Peter heard a sound to which he would give new voice. Peter listened anew to his own record collection, finding trace examples of a punk-cabaret crossover in Christian Death's "Lament" and Nick Cave and the Bad Seeds' "The Carney." In 1993, Robert Pinsky's translation of Dante's Inferno appeared on the shelves of St. Marks Bookshop and F.M. Einheit released Radio Inferno. In Dante, Peter had found a gothic touchstone moored in a familiar Italian Catholic imaginary. A sci-fi nerd who took special delight in absurd plot twists, Peter also read Stanislaw Lem, whose book, Futurological Congress, influenced the name of his new music project: The World/Inferno Friendship Society. At last, he had sound and concept with which to create an aesthetic domain thick enough to live in.

On November 26, 1995, the first World/Inferno show was held at Ciel Rouge, a bar with a distinctly pre-War vibe set off by Adrian, from The Wandering Dragon, its bartender. I'd estimate that about twenty souls were in attendance. Always generous, especially when it came to libation, Peter bought enough jugs of wine to sink a pirate ship. The show was convened by his slamming together a pair of tiny cymbals. He sang and Scott Hollingsworth played piano—that was the whole band.

Around this time, Peter became friends with a namesake who was a regular at The Continental: Peter King. Two people sharing the same name in a tiny scene was an annoyance, and Peter King was not going to be the one to change. In playful annoyance, Peter King called him "Jack." It was also, conveniently, the name of one of his favorite musicians, Jack Grisham of TSOL, who had, himself, taken stage names. Taking this as an invitation to assume a *nome d'arte*, a character to inhabit the domain he was creating, Peter accepted the name "Jack," and was given the "Terricloth" surname by Scott, who thought that Peter's voice sounded "big and fluffy... like terrycloth." Soon after, Peter King was struck and killed by a taxi outside The Continental in front of everyone, but the nickname stuck nonetheless.

Insert to World/Inferno Live at North Six

Over the next ensuing years, the World/Inferno grew into a full-on band, made records, and toured extensively. Every year since 1997, the World/Inferno played a show on Hallowmas, the night after Halloween, and each time they'd play a trick on their audience. I was deputized for a few Hallowmas capers. In 2001, just before the band was to go on stage at the Good/Bad Art Collective, Jack handed me a bottle of 141-proof rum, telling me "You can hit it, but not too hard because I'm going to need it later." At the end of the show, the band played a march and Jack signaled to me over the audience to follow him. He led the crowd out of the venue. In the middle of a parking lot there hung an effigy of Jack (or was it Peter?) dangling from a gallows. He climbed a ladder beside the gallows and gave me the high sign. I approached and handed him the rum. He took a mean swig, doused the effigy in drink, and set it aflame, which was an incredible spectacle to behold. The insert to the Live at North Six CD has a photo of it in which I'm beside him, staring straight up positively gobsmacked by what I saw.

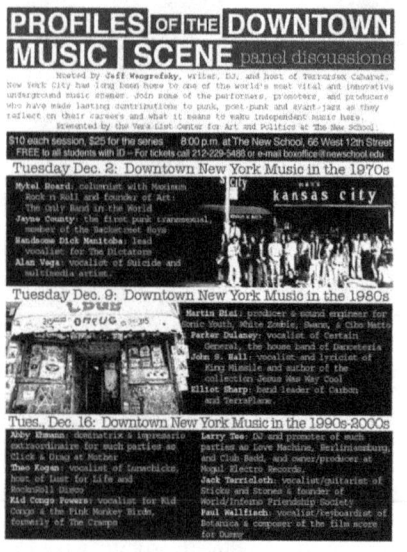

Courtesy JW

In the decades to follow, Jack and I continued to periodically get together for booze and schmooze at World/Inferno shows, at episodic parties at my place (S.H.I.T. in the Parlour), while seeing friends' bands, and randomly, on subway trains.

He was also a participant in a retrospective on the downtown NYC music scene I hosted at The New School as well as TerrorSex Cabaret, a monthly showcase of weird and slightly spooky acts that I curated for a year at Club Luxx in Brooklyn, and he was a guest on Gift Horse: Inside New York Art, a podcast series I hosted on Ukrainian radio for a year with Leslie Hodgkins. Jack also enlisted me, as an actor, in many World/Inferno antics, right up to the very last World/Inferno show.

***

While horrified and emotionally gutted by Jack's passing, it was not a complete shock, as he prided himself on living hard, as celebrated in many of his songs. A self-consuming artifact, he lived so hard that it surprised himself that he had lived to the half-century mark. Jack belonged to the strain of artists who use drugs to escape the traps of rationality, magnify the moment, and open himself and his art to chance and danger. This, it can be said, is the Johnny Thunders Church of Hunger Artistry, in which the performer, in full guise, lives out the Dionysian fantasies of the audience. It's not uncommon for such artists and their personae to be locked in a lethal embrace (e.g., Alfred Jarry). Unless somehow contained, the persona vampirically kills its corporeal host.

Sure, I partied with Jack at Brownie's, Kokie's, and other pre-morning narco-lounges, but I was a mere piker, whereas he took it as holy communion. I recall him sticking a straw into a bag of cocaine, snorting its contents all at once, and, soon after, repeating the feat, which seemed Paul Bunyan-esque even in that moment. Eventually, he gave up doing coke before performing as he'd forget the words, although, in his final few years, he'd often forget them anyway. About ten years back, he called me with heart palpitations, asking me to stay with him on the phone until someone brought him to a hospital. By his last few years, he became discernibly twitchy—too unsteady to write legibly, let alone craft lyrics—and appeared to age at an accelerated rate.

As for living into his dotage, he often professed both a desire to quit when he'd accomplished his goals as well as a persistent discomfort with becoming a nostalgia act. I recall a half-joking conversation Peter and I had with friends around 1993 at Dojo on St. Marks Place. As I was then approaching the grand old age of twenty-seven, he led the charge to convince me to kill myself at or before age thirty—the outer limit of the punk rock youth club. Some of the most honest things we say are in jest and song, you know. As he wrote in "Tattoos Fade": "There's not a thing I'd wish [would] last forever."

Liquor stores were among the very few businesses allowed to operate during the pandemic lockdown. Like so many isolated, dispirited people during those bewildering times, his vices got the better of him. At the same time, I bought a pair of sneakers and sweats, and took up running for the first time in my life, knowing that this was something Jack would not have done. We sink or we swim.

Before his transformation into Jack Terricloth, Peter told me that he'd much prefer being famous to being rich, provided it was on his terms, and he was convinced that others would eventually cash in on his approach to music. Living for better than twenty years cheek-to-jowl with Williamsburg hipsters, he never courted them as audience, never made dance music, and largely avoided modish nightspots. Instead, he preferred playing punk hangouts (initially only those with pianos), and developed a distinct fan base that gravitated to his charisma, abundant vocal talents, deft songwriting, and peculiar sensibility. Watching him make reality from his vision—a little subculture, with hordes of acolytes the world over—was miraculous, like watching a flower bloom. Instead of seeing Peter as an artist who created a body of work, I think of him as someone who did his utmost to craft an aesthetic life-world within which he was a musician. He made his life into art and invited others to join him, and some did.

This chapter is dedicated to dear friends who died during the pandemic lockdown—none from the disease: Leslie Barany, Suzette Bronkhorst, Ronald Eissens, Hash Halper, Larry Kessler, and Peter (of course).

Take the Last Train to Auschwitz: The Trouble with Trains

What is next in this sequence -
72, 79, 96, 103, 110 ?

Like two million other lost but busy souls, I take the New York City subway to and from work, and often on evenings and weekends as well. Over the decades, I've spent so much money on these trains I sometimes reckon that I've earned my initials on a grimy tile on the wall of the Delancey Street F station. Upon calculation, however, with over five million rides on an average weekday, my personal contribution is so miniscule, truly a token entry, that it can serve as a piquant reminder of my generally insignificant role in this earthly flea circus. With a whopping 472 stations spread between 27 lines that, together, stretch 691 miles of steel, Gotham's underbelly is exceptionally well-girded. The greater part of the subway system is, indeed, subterreanean, a parallel dimension beneath the city's concrete and asphalt skin, never exposed to the sun. The whole system has been in slow but discernible decay for a decade, slouching steadily into filth, inefficiency, and violence. It's heartbreaking and stupefying to see my beloved city lapsing toward ruin twice in my lifetime: the first, a tragedy, and the second, by design.

The subway is, of course, only one of several City-wide circulatory networks, with communication, electrical, steam, and sewage comprising the full complement. As the cheapest, simplest, and normally fastest form of transit, traversing the underworld is among the signature experiences of life in The City, a given period that city folk automatically lose, in addition to sleeptime and pooptime.

Subways are a domain at once unsupervised and

unfree. Entrances, now largely without token clerks, rely on an honor system that turns passengers into chumps and cheats while feeding a creeping financial and spiritual decrepitude—an immoral economy. Do you trust yourself to do the right thing when other people don't? Subway car interiors are the only public places I know in New York City without cameras. Electro-eyes stare out from nearly every building, and they record every trifling motion and emotion in corridors, stairwells, and elevators within. Stores of all sorts observe their customers, who sometimes waltz out with stolen items, nonetheless. Even busses and taxis spy on their riders, but trains roll on, outside official purview (which is great until it's not).

Data on train service is carefully crafted or suppressed. Suicides in the subway, for example, are largely unreported, known only to the dead's close friends and family, only faintly intimated in the ether and in dreams. We don't really know how many distraught souls, unable to fulfil their purpose in life, sacrifice their bodies to the stainless-steel Moloch each spring and around the equinox, hurtling with hearts pounding, into grinding mutilation, and onward into oblivion.

***

My first train trips were *in utero*. My dear, departed mother, all five-foot two of her, took the train to work when she was pregnant with me. As the train rattled, halted abruptly, and lurched back into motion, again and again, as it still does, my egg was scrambled. Tucked up in her primordial snugness, I had my first lesson in the apparently random jerk-and-flow of life.

When I was a little kid, with the old wheels and brakes, experiencing a train entering a station was like being overtaken by a giant wave. First came a cone of particulates from the tracks pushed before the oncoming colossus—rat hair, poop of all kinds, dust, mites, and the vast array of microbial critters peculiar to the subway which have yet evaded scientific taxonomy. This was followed by tremors I have grown too callous from life to feel any longer. And, finally, with a cry of steel wheels on steel tracks grinding in fevered static, so enormous—stentorian—that it registered as a vision of white-hot sparks engulfing the entirety of the platform, the train pulled into view.

Nowadays my workday migration begins with a hike through NYC's Lower East Side and Chinatown. Plummeting two flights into darkness, I enter the station. New York City subway trains are named after letters and numbers without descriptive purchase on the geography they cross. I wade into the alphabet soup of letters without words and numbers without math: D or B trains to Atlantic Avenue-Barclays Center, a transfer for the 4 or 5 train to Franklin Avenue, and the 3 train to the Kingston Avenue Crown Heights.

In all, my five-mile trek takes anywhere from 35 minutes to an hour or more, and there is no way of knowing beforehand which it will be. Once aboard, excuses or not, I'm tied to the tracks, so to say, committed to a path. Delays in transit can happen at any and all legs of the sojourn. And when given explanations, they often appear suspect or absurd.

**

Small white eyes gleam from a distance, and soon, a train enters—an enormous worm stretching across the platform and expelling people from its belly. I shuffle in, accepting fate at the dodgy crossroads of public policy and technology.

There are a few classic styles of subway riding: couples seated astride one other; teenagers putting their feet on seats; some sit alone, reading, listening to music, fixed to phones, or doing nothing at all; and the surfers. I am a surfer: I stand in doorways because I sit far too much as it is and because I don't relish contact with seats that are never cleaned. Whenever possible, I eschew the handrails, which are also never cleaned. Never ever. Microscopy would reveal it all covered in dead skin, urine, feces, rat hair, food, and whatever else anyone could never want to touch or brush against. There are also some formal and informal behavioral expectations reflecting the shared, public nature of mass transit: don't eat (which makes an unsanitary place even less sanitary); don't blast music (which is rude and egoistical); don't fall asleep (both unsafe and likely to miss your stop); don't touch anyone (unless invited); don't talk to strangers (Stanley Milgram contrived studies on it); and monitor the antics of "showtime" with sidelong glances to avoid being kicked in the head. Of course, these "rules" are sometimes violated, and when they are, it often signals trouble. Most people, enjoying a few private moments before work or without family in an overcrowded and overheated city, sit silently, up in their heads, simply wanting to be left alone.

Sometimes the train is delayed when I first get on board, its doors incontinently leaking cool air conditioning while the humid stink of Chinatown in the summer wades in. Trains often stop moving while on the Manhattan Bridge. There, suspended 135 feet above the East River, the car—an enormous canister of steel and plastic and human meat—squeaks to a crawl and then fully halts. From above and to the side, this view of the city is a treat for the eyes, and the East River provides additional scenic distraction with water-taxi hydrofoils, tugs, tankers and other cargo ships, yachts and schooners, police boats, and jet skis cutting across the estuary. Cue the music, care of David Bowie's "Space Oddity": *"I'm sitting in a tin can/far above the world/The river is a slimy green/and I'm caught in between."*

Then, moving once again, we slide into a tunnel leading below Brooklyn. Then inside the tunnel, there are often additional delays as dispatchers—the ghosts in the machine—determine, from some unseen nexus, whether my B or D train should precede or succeed an N or R train merging onto the same tracks. I might imagine that coordinating trains would be simple. After all, they move slowly, in a single direction, toward pre-set termini. I conjecture as to what combination of beguiling complexity, technological inadequacy, or gross inefficiency in workers and/or management is keeping me from my job that moment. The length and frequency of the delays suggest different "weightings" of complexity, inadequacy, or inefficiency to feed my bug-a-boos. The tracks, so certain in their direction and destination, are spooked by spirits that cannot be easily propitiated or appeased, let alone understood. Haven't you ever wanted to know how it all works?

Like every other schnook sporting an increasingly skeletal face, I'm yet another blinkered rider paying a fare, unable to know train delays and detours for what they are, forever unable to distinguish dream from reality, and hard-wired to the same foolish mistakes again and then some. Once aboard, I surrender all but the most subtle agency, as much hostage as passenger. Time becomes local and discernibly relative. Language and mathematics, unmoored from meaning, swirl randomly. Each moment of waiting in this netherworld, as measured in minutes or seconds, stretches on for hours or even whole days in the world above, pointing toward eternity, as the infinity between numbers is as great as the infinity among them. If I am fated to arrive at work at 9:40 instead of 9:00, as per my wont, who am I to grind against the grain? Byron Nease, when I was his personal assistant, about a year before he succumbed to AIDS, would sometimes offer reassuring perspective on the petty tyrannies of existence: "The great thing about life is that you cannot lose."

***

At each station, people enter and leave the trains, shuffling and reshuffling the deck with chance meetings across eight to eleven cars spread across hundreds of feet. The odds of any particular pairing of people are low, though the effect of these mixtures of personalities are integral to the trip and sometimes much more. As Donny the Punk would say, "It's not the time, it's the company." Over the decades, I've ridden the rails with stars and celebrities, many unrecognized out of context, though I have seen a few (Don Mattingly, Philip Glass, Leonard Lopate, Michael "The Illustrated Man" Wilson). Of course there were also exotic creatures as well, people I've only seen underground, and can hardly imagine existing in the world above. Back in the late 1980s and early '90s, with violence and decay in full bloom, a black fella without legs would ride between cars on a skateboard with a coffee can, begging for spare change along with the rest of the broken metropolis. What became of him I leave to your speculation.

Once at Atlantic Avenue-Barclays Center, I hustle up a flight of stairs, across a hall, dodging columns and slow-moving pedestrians, down two flights and back up two to transfer to the 4 or 5 train. Even for an express, the ride to Franklin Avenue is long, and often selected by people wishing to perpetrate sadistic exploits, opportunistic thievery, or acts of hatred—some lethal.

In December 2019, I transferred at Atlantic Avenue and got on a train empty except for a very large black guy, about half my age, with short hair, wearing a down vest. As a subway "surfer," I stood in the doorway, as is my way, across from him with about ten feet between us, when the door closed.

He commanded: "I don't like Jewish people. You need to move."

Still barking at dogs, I matter-of-factly replied, "I most certainly will not."

While there are times when I dress more or less "Jewish," my conspicuously Jewish proboscis always precedes me, announcing my ethnicity, my history, my blood, to people hunting for Homo Judaicum. In sixth grade, kids threw pennies at me in class. In high school, I was shown caricatures in which I was depicted as a pelican, and some kids sung lyrics at me to the tune of Black Sabbath's "Iron Man" (a song of revenge I was keen on then): *"Jeff Wengrofsky's a Jew/ we eat steak/he eats stew. Jeff Wengrofsky's a queer/when he's around/no one's near."* And, sure, I faced episodic intimidation from demented students and bigoted faculty during my last years of graduate school, but it never actually turned physical. This was going to be one of those times—or much worse.

Rising to his feet, slowly unfurling his vast height, far taller and beefier than he had appeared while seated, he walked to me, and extending his hand to my chest, pushed me slowly backward, gently but firmly, for about ten or fifteen feet, toward to the middle of the train. Drawing on epigenetic and lived experience, I knew better than to vocally protest or resist, instead moving in response with his physical suggestions. He then returned to his seat, and I sat down on a bench where he had pushed me. Hoping that sitting in my assigned place, far away, would appease him, I was disconcerted to hear a tirade of insults and accusations about Jews, outrageous and ridiculous things, culminating in his denouncing me as a "Jew devil." Although I'd heard Black Israelites call me a "devil," it was always with other people around. And, years later, when I taught, I even had a student declare through gold grills that he looked forward to "'The Final Call,' when we'll kill all y'all," but it wasn't personal. In contrast, this was a tangibly direct encounter without a witness, an exit option, or bail to protect me from my assailant—if I lived to press charges.

He stood again and moved my way. This time I pointed my phone at him to record events. Turning his back to my camera to hide his face, he stood in the doorway. Resuming his demonizing harangue, he spun again, stepping toward me, motioning—eyes wide in fury—as if he would try to grab my phone or worse. But for whatever reason, he abruptly thought the better of it. Blood percolated thick and fast in my ears. Just then, the train pulled into the Franklin Avenue station. Turning again, he ducked through the train doorway and swept up the stairs and out of my life. I transferred at Franklin and exited the subway at Kingston Avenue, emerging into the light of day.

Prayer for the Solitary Subway Rider

I call upon my Guardian and Light
to ride beside me on this perilous journey.
Remember me, as Noah was remembered.
Help me understand, as with Job.
Deliver my body and provide succor to my Soul.
If this is the last train to Auschwitz,
please meet me at the station.
I don't want to go this way alone.
Oh, no, no, no.
And I don't know if I'm ever going home.

(Repeat as necessary.)

ALSO OUT ON FAR WEST

SONNY VINCENT — Snake Pit Therapy

BRENT L. SMITH — Pipe Dreams on Pico

JOSEPH MATICK — The Baba Books

KURT EISENLOHR — Stab the Remote

KANSAS BOWLING — A Cuddly Toys Companion

KANSAS BOWLING & PARKER LOVE BOWLING — Prewritten Letters for Your Convenience

CRAIG DYER — Heavier Than a Death in the Family

PARKER LOVE BOWLING — Rhododendron, Rhododendron

JENNIFER ROBIN — You Only Bend Once with a Spoonful of Mercury

JOSEPH MATICK — Cherry Wagon

RICHARD CABUT — Disorderly Magic

NORMAN DOUGLAS — Love and the Fear of Love

ELIZABETH ELLEN — Estranged

farwestpress.com

+1 (541) FAR-WEST

Printed in the USA
CPSIA information can be obtained
at www.ICGtesting.com
JSHW022326120923
48368JS00005B/31

9 798985 806786